081439

H   Hoban, Julia
             Quick Chick.

9.95

Library of Congress Cataloging-in-Publication Data
Hoban, Julia.   *89 B13004*
  Quick Chick.
  (Dutton easy reader)
  Summary: Although he seems much slower than
the other chicks, Jenny Hen's youngest chick
finally earns his name—Quick Chick.
  [1. Chickens—Fiction] I. Hoban, Lillian,
ill. II. Title III. Series.
PZ7.H63487Qu 1989 [E] 88-30894
ISBN 0-525-44490-4

Published in the United States by
E. P. Dutton, New York, N.Y.,
a division of NAL Penguin Inc.
Published simultaneously in Canada by
Fitzhenry & Whiteside Limited, Toronto
Printed in Hong Kong
First Edition   10 9 8 7 6 5 4 3 2 1

for Frank, the best chick

J.H.

It was early morning.

Jenny Hen was sitting on her nest.

"Good morning, Jenny Hen,"

said Alice Pig.

"Good morning,"

said Jenny Hen.

"Have you met my little chicks?

This is Cute Chick,

Sweet Chick,

and Good Chick."

"But you are still sitting on an egg,"

said Alice.

"Yes," said Jenny Hen.

"This will be Nice Chick."

"Hatch, Nice Chick," said Jenny Hen.

"Hatch quickly. Then all my little chicks

can learn their lessons together."

Chip chip! The egg cracked.

Two black, beady eyes

peeped over the shell.

Slowly a chick climbed out.

Then he sat down.

"You see," said Jenny Hen.

"He is a nice chick."

"He may be a nice chick,"

said Alice Pig.

"But he is *very* slow.

Maybe you should

call him Slow Chick."

"Just you wait and see,"

said Jenny Hen.

First Jenny Hen taught

her little chicks to scratch for corn.

Cute Chick and Sweet Chick did it.

So did Good Chick.

But the last chick did not.

He scratched once to the right.

He scratched once to the left.

Then he stopped and looked around.

"What dear little chicks,"

said Mabel Goat.

"But why won't the littlest one scratch?"

"He will," said Jenny Hen.

"My chicks will all learn their lessons."

"But when?" said Mabel.

"He is so slow.

Maybe you should call him Slow Chick."

"Just you wait and see,"

said Jenny Hen.

Next Jenny Hen taught

her little chicks

to dig for worms.

Cute Chick and Sweet Chick did it.

So did Good Chick.

But the last chick did not.

He dug to the right.

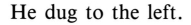

He dug to the left.

Then he watched the clouds go by.

"Oh! Such sweet chicks,"

said Lucy Duck.

"But why won't the littlest one dig?"

"He will," said Jenny Hen.

"My chicks will all learn their lessons."

"But when?" said Lucy.

"I think you should call

him Slow Chick."

"Just you wait and see,"

said Jenny Hen.

Next Jenny Hen

taught her little chicks

to peck for seeds.

Cute Chick and Sweet Chick did it.

So did Good Chick.

But the last chick did not.

He pecked to the right.

He pecked to the left.

Then he stopped and yawned.

"Oh, my chick," said Jenny Hen.

"You must learn to peck

like all little chicks."

"What cute chicks,"

said Betty Lamb.

"But why won't the littlest one peck?"

"He will," said Jenny Hen.

"My chicks will all learn their lessons."

"But when?" said Betty.

"He is so slow.

Don't you think

you should call him Slow Chick?"

"Just you wait and see,"

said Jenny Hen.

Then Jenny Hen taught her little chicks

to clean their feathers.

Cute Chick and Sweet Chick did it.

So did Good Chick.

But the last chick did not.

He plucked on his right side.

He plucked on his left side.

Then he tucked his head

under his wing and went to sleep.

"Oh dear," said Jenny Hen

to Millie Cow.

"My last chick will not

learn his lessons."

Then Jenny Hen said to her chicks,

"This is the most important lesson.

On this farm there is a cat.

So follow close behind me

in a straight line.

Then the cat will not get you."

"Yes," said Millie Cow.

"Cats are very fond

of chasing little chicks."

Jenny Hen started walking.

Cute Chick and Sweet Chick

followed her.

So did Good Chick.

But the last chick did not.

He took one step on his right foot.

He took one step on his left foot.

Then he sat down.

"Look out, Slow Chick!"

called Alice Pig and Mabel Goat

and Lucy Duck and Betty Lamb

and Millie Cow.

"Here comes the cat."

The chick looked behind him.

He saw a big cat.

It had a long tail.

It had lots of pointy teeth.

The chick picked up his right foot.

He picked up his left foot.

Then he ran.

He ran very fast.

He did not look at the clouds.

He did not yawn or go to sleep.

He ran and ran.

The cat ran right behind him.

The chick ran to the creek.

Then he stopped running.

But the cat did not stop.

The cat went—*splash!*—

right into the creek.

"Yeow!" cried the cat.

"That is some quick chick,"

said everyone.

"I told you all along,"

said Jenny Hen.

That afternoon, Sammy Dog

met Jenny Hen's chicks.

"This is Cute Chick,

Sweet Chick,

and Good Chick," said Jenny.

"What is the littlest one's name?"

asked Sammy.

Jenny Hen said,

"The littlest one is named

QUICK CHICK."